Pop Flop's Great Balloon Ride

by Nancy Abruzzo

Illustrations by Noel Chilton

The author acknowledges Don Usner for his editorial
and storyline assistance.

Manufactured in Canada
10 9 8 7 6 5 4 3 2 1

Library of Congress Cataloging-in-Publication Data

Abruzzo, Nancy
  Pop Flop's great balloon ride / by Nancy Abruzzo ; illustrations by
Noel Chilton.
      p. cm.
  Summary: Mary Pat sends one of her stuffed animals for a ride in her
father's hot air balloon at the Albuquerque Balloon Fiesta.
  ISBN 0-89013-475-8 (paper over boards : alk. paper)
[1. Hot air balloons—Fiction. 2. Toys—Fiction. 3. Albuquerque
(N.M.)—Fiction.] I. Chilton, Noel, ill. II. Title.
  PZ7.A17285Pop 2005
  [E]—dc22
                                    2005007425

Museum of New Mexico Press
Post Office Box 2087
Santa Fe, New Mexico 87504
www.mnmpress.org

In memory of our
dear friend
Marc Sevrin,
who shared his love
and passion for
ballooning
with so many.

It's a cold, early October morning in Albuquerque.

Mary Pat and Rico, and their cousins Nicoy and Robert,
are all together for the weekend to enjoy the Balloon Fiesta.

"Up, up, up! It's time to go see the balloons!" whispers Mama.

"Oh, but it's still dark—it's not morning yet!" yawns Nicoy.
"And baby Rico is still asleep." "Babies need lots of sleep, but you're a big girl
and I know you can get up," says Mama.

"Do I have to wear this jacket?" asks Mary Pat. "I'm so *hot*!"

"You'll be glad you have it when we're outside at the balloon park," Mama assures Mary Pat.

"And Robert, put on this hat."

"I don't see any balloons," exclaims Robert, looking up to the sky.

"Don't worry, soon we'll see more balloons than you can count," Mama replies.

"I see fire in the sky!" shouts Nicoy.

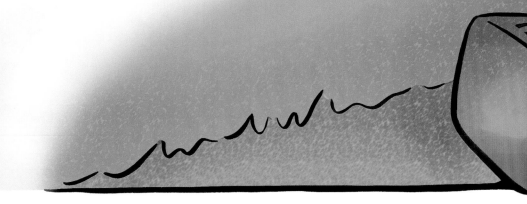

"I've seen this before," says Mary Pat. "That's the dawn patrol.
Those balloons go up when it's still dark!"

"Let's see who's first to find Daddy's balloon," says Mama.

"I see Daddy by the balloon!" yells Mary Pat.
"Let's hurry so we can help him inflate it."
"But there's fire over there!" says Nicoy.
"It looks like dragon's breath."

"Silly, there's no dragon," says Mary Pat.
"The flames come from the burners that heat the air.
This makes the balloons float in the sky."
"That's right, Mary Pat, we're safe," Mama assures them.

"Look!" points Robert, "I see a bumble bee balloon."
"And a bear balloon too," shouts Nicoy.

"Daddy, Daddy!" says Mary Pat. "Are you almost ready to fly?
Can I go with you? I'm not scared."
"Not this time, Mary Pat. You went yesterday," says Daddy.
"Now you and Robert and Nicoy stay close to Mama."

"And remember, there will be a loud sound and flames when Daddy uses the burner,"
explains Mama.

"Why is that man in the zebra suit blowing his whistle and pointing his thumb in the ai[r]" asks Robert. "He's the launch director," replies Mama.

"That means it's Daddy's turn to fly!" says Mary Pat. "All balloonists must wait their tur[n]

Suddenly Mary Pat calls out, "Wait, Daddy, wait! Can Pop Flop go up with you? He wants to go!"

"Yes, hurry," calls Daddy.

"How many balloons do you see now?" asks Mama.

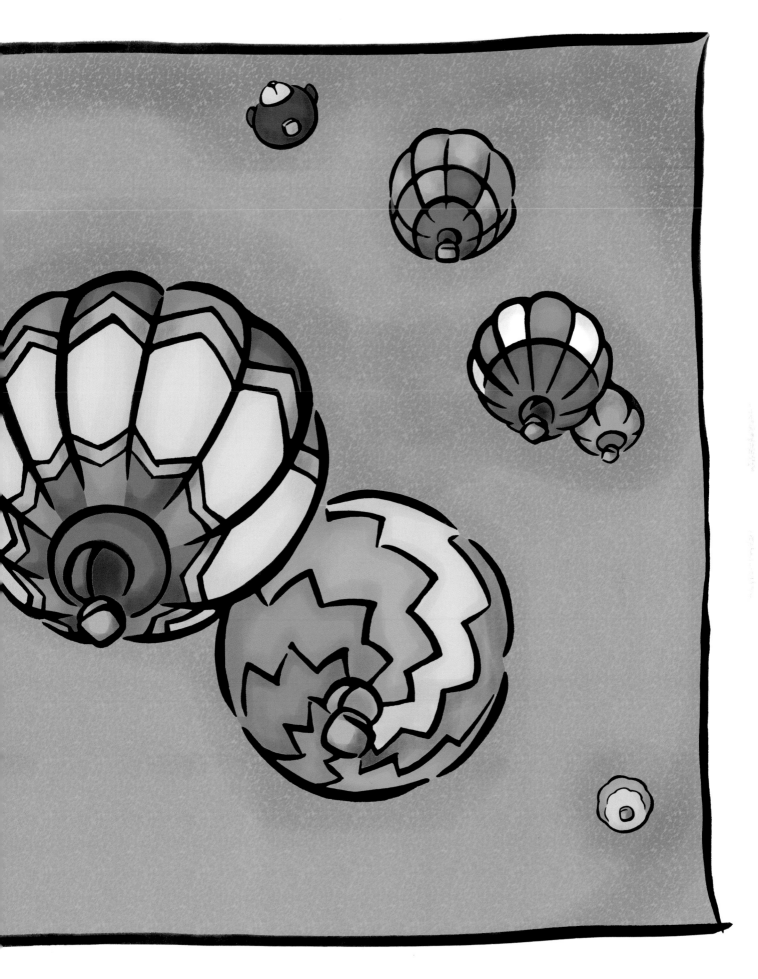

"One, two, three, four . . . I can't count all of them!" laughs Nicoy.

"I wonder if Pop Flop is having fun?" says Robert.

"I think so, he gets to see everything," says Nicoy.

"Do you think Pop Flop can see us?" asks Nicoy?

"I bet we look as small as ants to him," says Mama.

"Maybe if we jump up and down he'll see us!" shouts Mary Pat.

"Pop Flop can see the whole world now!" says Robert.

"Well, at least all of Albuquerque," Mama replies.

"Won't the flames from the burner hurt Pop Flop?" Nicoy wonders.

"No," Mary Pat replies. "All the heated air goes up into the balloon.
That's what makes it rise. My daddy told me."

"Will Uncle Richard and Pop Flop ever come down?"
asks Robert.

"They're so far away!"

"Yes, they will, Robert," says Mama.
"Uncle Richard will land the balloon safely and we'll see them at home."

"Now, who wants some hot cocoa?"

"I do! I do! I do!" yell the children.

"Mama! I can't wait until Daddy gets home.
I want to see Pop Flop and ask him about his ride in the balloon," says Mary Pat.

"Well, it's our lucky day, Mary Pat. Do you see Grandpa in his truck over there?
Grandpa's going to pick up Daddy and his balloon. We can follow him."

"There they are! There they are!" shouts Mary Pat.

"Pop Flop! Daddy! Was it fun?
Did you see me waving at you?" shouts Mary Pat.

"We saw you when we took off. And Pop Flop thoug[ht]
about you the whole flight," says Daddy.
"I'm sure he'll tell you all about it tonight."

"Yes, but now it's home for a nap," says Mama.
"Look, baby Rico is still sleeping! He missed all the
balloons," Mary Pat says, laughing.

, Pop Flop," says Mary Pat. "I can't wait to hear about
ur great balloon ride! And I'll tell Rico all about it."